Daisy Sea

Buccaneer Cove

Long Tail Lake

Chocolate Mountain

Chipped Mouth Village

Squid Cape

Skull Islet

To the small and wonderful crew that cheers my days.
To Mom and Dad; thank you for teaching me to
always navigate with my heart in my hand.
Finally, to you; without you
there would have been no beginning...

Alicia Acosta

With love to you. For a life full of adventures!

Mónica Carretero

Little Captain Jack
Somos8 Series

© Text: Alicia Acosta, 2016
© Illustrations: Mónica Carretero, 2016
© Edition: NubeOcho, 2017
www.nubeocho.com – info@nubeocho.com

Original title: *El pequeño pirata Serafín*
Translated by Martin Hyams and Charlotte Hyams
Text editing: Caroline Dookie, Kim Griffin and Teddi Rachlin.

Distributed in the United States by
Consortium Book Sales & Distribution

First edition: 2017
ISBN: 978-84-945415-0-6
Printed in China

LITTLE CAPTAIN JACK

Alicia Acosta
Mónica Carretero

nubeOCHO

Once upon a time there was a **little** pirate. He was so very little that everyone called him **Little Captain Jack**.

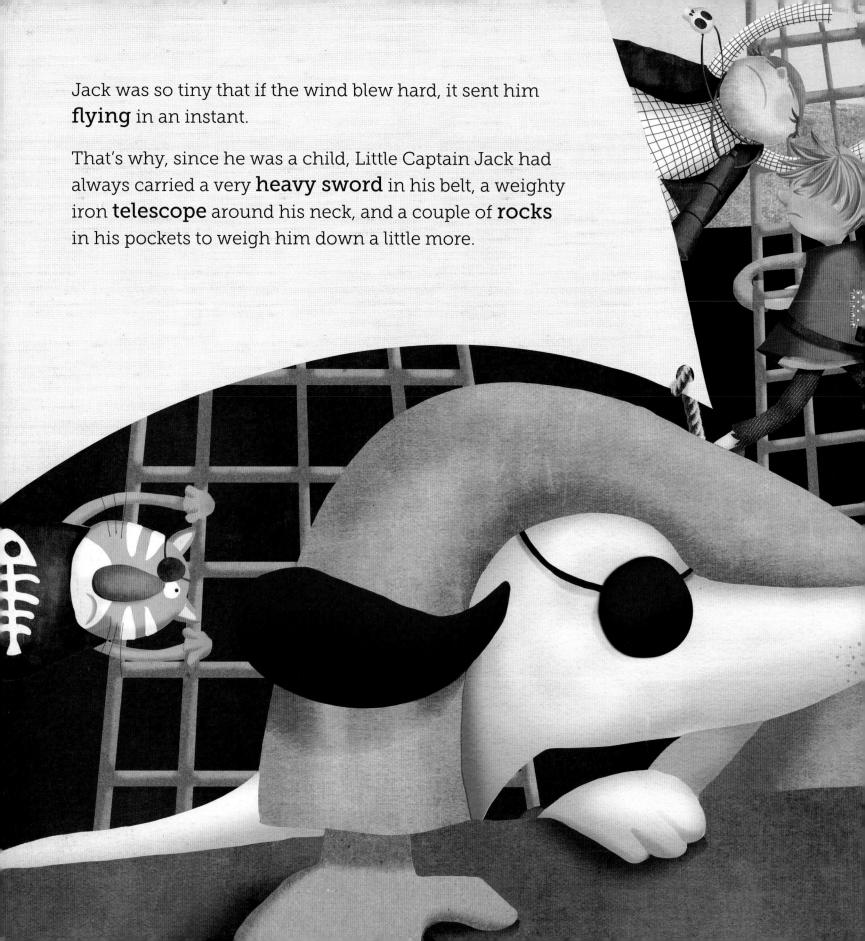

Jack was so tiny that if the wind blew hard, it sent him **flying** in an instant.

That's why, since he was a child, Little Captain Jack had always carried a very **heavy sword** in his belt, a weighty iron **telescope** around his neck, and a couple of **rocks** in his pockets to weigh him down a little more.

The pirate's size was also a problem at work. Jack was so tiny that his crew didn't **hear** him even when he **yelled** at them.

So when he said, **"Come on you sea dogs!"** the crew heard **"Get on your flip-flops!"** and ran off to get their **bathing suits** and **beach towels** to head off to the beach.

If Little Captain Jack said: "Bring out the paddles!"
his crew would hear "Blow out the candles!" and they would
bring out the candles, start singing *Happy birthday to you*,
and then blow them out as if they were on a cake.

If Little Captain Jack shouted: **"Batten down the hatches!"** they'd hear **"Butter the ham sandwiches!"** and run to the kitchen to stuff themselves with ham sandwiches.

Little Captain Jack was **tired** of always having to be careful that he didn't get trampled into a **flapjack**. He was **fed up** with being so **small**, always having to be vigilant, always having to yell:

Careful! I'm here! Careful! I'm there!

In the end, he invented a
little **ditty** that he always repeated
whenever he needed to:

Careful now,
watch your back,
here comes Little Captain Jack!

One day, well, one **terrible day** actually,
Little Captain Jack was in the middle of a battle with
other pirates. As he fought, he said the ditty from time
to time, so that no one would tread on him:

Careful now,
watch your back,
here comes Little Captain Jack!

Suddenly, Pirate **Badlock**, a bad pirate, **as bad as they come**, heard the little song, looked down with his **one eye**, and laughed to himself. He picked up Little Captain Jack with two fingers and stuffed him in his pocket.

Pirate Badlock, a bad pirate, as bad as they come, was very **tall**, so although Jack could get out of the pocket, it was too **dangerous** to jump down to the ground.

Pirate Badlock took Little Captain Jack to his ship and locked him in a deep, dark **cellar**. There was no way of **escaping** as the steps were too **high** for Jack to climb.

The little pirate began to **cry**, thinking he would never get back to his crew. Then a **small mouse** that lived in that dark place, approached him and asked:

"What kind of mouse are you? And why are you crying?"

Jack told the mouse the full story and said he missed his **crew**.

"**Don't worry!**" the little mouse said, "Don't cry. I'll get you out of here. Get on my back!"

The mouse was so **tiny** that it slipped through the cracks in the floorboards and took him up to the open deck.

But when Captain Jack emerged and looked from the ship's **bow**, he saw that they were surrounded by water.

"What now?" said Jack. "How will I get back to my boat? I am so small... I can't **row** or **swim**. **The fish will eat me!**"

The little mouse **whistled** loudly, far up to the clouds, and almost immediately **Sophie the Seagull**, the little mouse's friend, appeared.

"Climb up, quick!" Sophie said,
knowing exactly what to do.

At first Little Captain Jack was **afraid**, clinging tightly to Sophie's feathers, then the feathers started to tickle him, and finally, he started to enjoy the ride. The more he enjoyed himself, the more his smile grew.

Captain Jack's crew was frantic. The **battle** was over.
They had searched everywhere but couldn't find their **captain**.

Everyone feared that he had been **eaten** by Pirate **Badlock**,
the bad pirate, as bad as they come.

When the **crew** saw Jack on the seagull, they wept with joy. They **hugged** him and, to celebrate his return, they threw a **party** —a small one but still, a party— and Little Captain Jack told them everything that had happened.

The sailors couldn't believe it. Their captain had been saved because he was so tiny that he could ride on a **mouse** and fly on a **seagull**!

From that day on, Little Captain Jack knew that **great things** could come in all shapes and sizes, **big** or **small**.

He never again complained about his size and he finally felt **proud** and **happy** to be Little Captain Jack!

PENNY ISLAND

Daisy Sea

Seagull Coast

Old Pirate Wood

N

NW

NE

W

E

SW

SE

S